The Adventures of

Magnus
the Dragonfly

Written and Illustrated
by Christine Renee Hourscht

To Phoebe
Enjoy life's adventures!
Christine

The Adventures of
Magnus the Dragonfly

ISBN: 9781980967118

Illustrations, Cover Art, & Interior Layout:
Christine Renee Hourscht
www.ChristineRenee.SquareSpace.com

Magnus the Dragonfly Song

Christine Hourscht

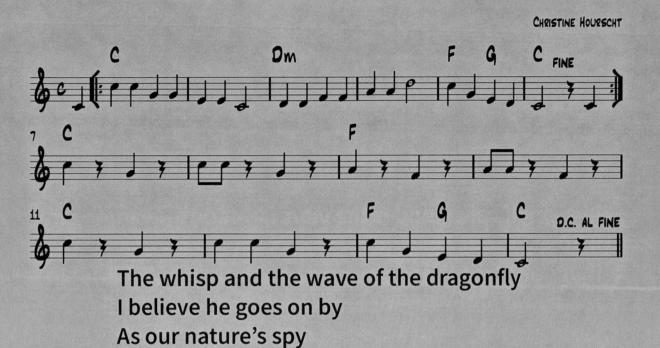

The whisp and the wave of the dragonfly
I believe he goes on by
As our nature's spy

He wanders with curiosity
He likes to fly by the lilies and the trees
And sometimes right by me

Dances, sings, waving his wings
He loves to fly way up high
Orange, green, yellow and blue
Colors he sees 'round you!

His adventures are with his friends
They meet and greet for lots of fun
In the rain or sun

He smiles and laughs while in the sky
Waving hello and goodbye
As he whisps on by

In a small valley under the vibrant moon and amongst 81,000 eucalyptus trees, there is a magnificent magnolia tree that no person has ever seen. This is the world of the mystical dragonflies, a world full of laughter, love, and sweet songs. Dragonflies dance through the air, whisping and waving in the sky.

Peering closely into the giant white flowers of the magnolia tree, you will see the dragonflies' houses. They are built with colorful leaves, branches, foliage and other natural materials. The large leaves of the magnolia tree shelter the homes from the wind and rain. Magnus lives in one of these houses in the magnolia tree. He is very smart, very wise and always very curious.

It is January and today is Magnus's birthday. His family is helping him celebrate his special day, a day he has been waiting a long, long time for. Today, he is old enough to get his wings! His mom and dad have been telling him bedtime stories about their winglife experiences every night before he goes to sleep. Soon, Magnus will have his own stories to tell about his new adventures.

On this early morning, Magnus looks out his window and sees his dear friend, Sierra the Bee. He smiles and winks at Sierra and she laughs. Magnus says, "Today is going to be a great day. I'm going to fly just like you." Sierra had been visiting Magnus every day in anticipation of his birthday. She loved to tell him stories about flying - actually, she mostly told him about the sweet fragrances of flowers - and that flying was awesome!

What a magical day this is, thought Magnus, as he ate his birthday cake. He opened his birthday card from his mom and dad. Inside was a map of their world!

Next, he opened his present to find his birthday wings.

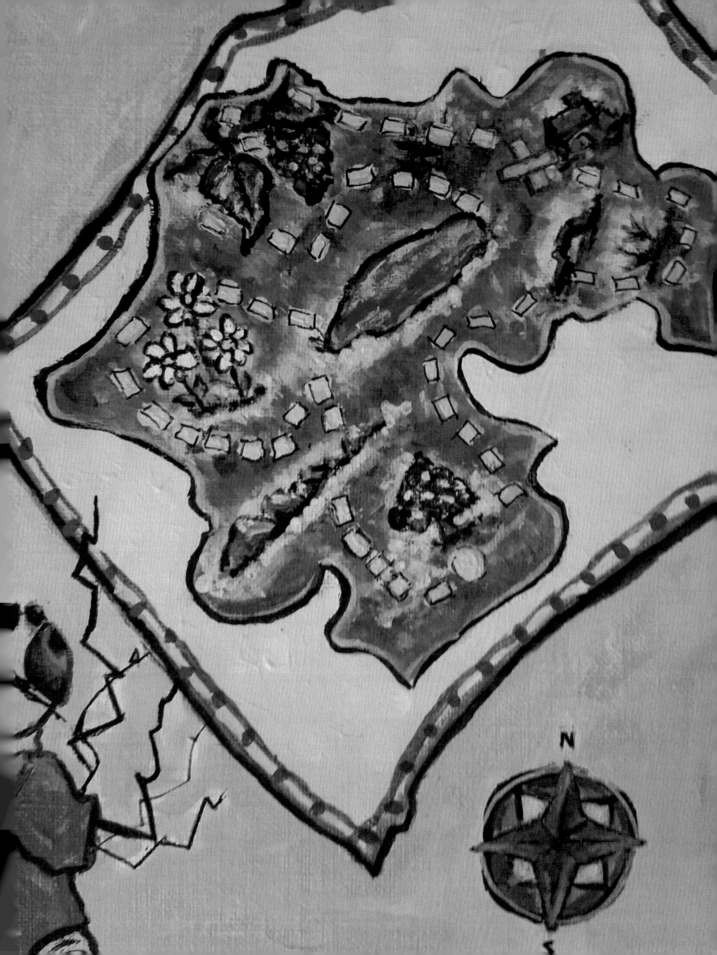

"These are so cool," Magnus said with excitement!

He then quickly put on his new wings. He and
Sierra set off into the sky on his first journey!

As they flew joyously in the sky, they noticed a wolf on some rocks near a log cabin. He smiled at them and said, "Hi, my name is Korbin the Wolf. It looks like you are having fun!"

Sierra the Bee began to sing:

MAGNUS THE DRAGONFLY SONG

CHRISTINE HOURSCHT

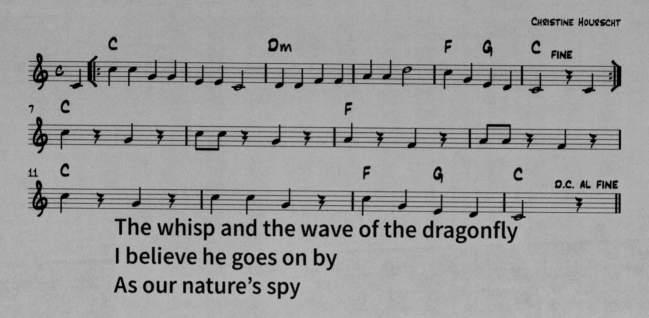

The whisp and the wave of the dragonfly
I believe he goes on by
As our nature's spy

He wanders with curiosity
He likes to fly by the lilies and the trees
And sometimes right by me

Dances, sings, waving his wings
He loves to fly way up high
Orange, green, yellow and blue
Colors he sees 'round you!

His adventures are with his friends
They meet and greet for lots of fun
In the rain or sun

He smiles and laughs while in the sky
Waving hello and goodbye
As he whisps on by

Whisping and waving with the wind as their friend, they saw a turtle in some foliage near a lake. She peeked through the leaves and said:

Next, they saw a rabbit hopping and laughing alongside some grapevines. As the bunny bounced, she said, "Hi, my name is Ashley the Rabbit. Do you love grapes too?"

As Magnus and Sierra turned around to go home, they saw an owl in a tree. He looked at them and quietly said, "Hoot! Hoot! My name is Austin the Owl. Who are you?"

Later that night after his most fantastic day EVER, Magnus told his mom and dad his first bedtime tale. He said he met new friends including Korbin the Wolf, Ashley the Rabbit, Austin the Owl, Jaeda the Turtle, a snake, and a woodpecker too. He gleefully said that he could not wait to put his wings on again!

When Magnus finally closed his eyes to sleep, he dreamed about more adventures to come. In his dreams, anything was possible. He was Magnus the Courageous, Magnus the Wise, Magnus the Strong. He was even Magnus the Incredible!

About the Author

Living in a small town in California, Christine Renee Hourscht is surrounded by nature's beauty. She likes to hike among the trees, admiring flowers, birds, and other animals. She is also enchanted by the ocean, lakes, insects, sky, and fresh air. It fills her with colorful inspiration.

As an artist, Christine is passionate about the beauty of life and lives in gratitude. Her artwork portrays this with whimsical movements, shapes and colors. Her philosophy is to "Live to love" and "Every breath we take is precious." Her artwork is a way to share moments in time.

One morning when a dragonfly whisped and waved near her face, the dragonfly song was born. Magnus's adventures began as Christine visited her favorite magnolia tree and when hiking in wine country.

Special Note from the Author

Dear Readers:
    Thank you for reading **The Adventures of Magnus the Dragonfly.** *This book is an introduction to many journeys for Magnus and his friends. I'm looking forward to sharing these with you soon!*

Christine

Made in the USA
San Bernardino, CA
06 October 2018